The Best of K'tonton

Other Books by Sadie Rose Weilerstein

What Danny Did

What the Moon Brought

The Singing Way: A Book of Verse for the Jewish Child

Little New Angel

Molly and the Sabbath Queen

Our Baby: A Record Book for the Jewish Child

Jewish Heroes

Dick, the Horse That Kept the Sabbath

Ten and a Kid

K'tonton Books

The Adventures of K'tonton

K'tonton in Israel

K'tonton on an Island in the Sea

K'tonton in the Circus: A Hanukkah Adventure

K'tonton's Sukkot Adventure

THE BEST OF

Illustrated by MARILYN HIRSH

Introduction by Francine Klagsbrun

THE JEWISH PUBLICATION SOCIETY

PHILADELPHIA

1980 · 5741

Sadie Rose Weilerstein

K'TONTON

*The greatest adventures in the
life of the Jewish thumbling,
K'tonton ben Baruch Reuben,
collected for the 50th anniversary
of his first appearance in print*

The Jewish Publication Society
2100 Arch Street, 2nd floor
Philadelphia, PA 19103

The stories in this collection, selected by the editors of The Jewish Publication Society,
are taken from the following books:
"K'tonton Arrives," "K'tonton Takes a Ride on a Chopping Knife and Wishes He
Hadn't," "K'tonton Goes to Synagogue and Swings on a *Lulav*," "K'tonton Takes a Ride on a
Runaway *Dreidel*," "K'tonton Masquerades on Purim," and "K'tonton Is Forgiven on Yom
Kippur" from *The Adventures of K'tonton*. Published by Women's League for Conservative
Judaism.

"K'tonton goes out into the Wide World," "Sabbath on the Island," "K'tonton Has a
Problem," "A Shavout Party on the Island," and "K'tonton leaves the Island" from *K'tonton on
an Island in the Sea*. Published by The Jewish Publication Society of America.

"K'tonton Goes to Israel," "K'tonton Goes up to Jerusalem," "A Passover Mix-Up,"
"Wisdom from a donkey," and "Size isn't Everything" from *K'tonton in Israel*. Published by
Women's League for Conservative Judaism.

Manufactured in the United States of America

Designed by Adrianne Onderdonk Dudden

Library of Congress Cataloging in Publication Data
Weilerstein, Sadie Rose, 1894-   The Best of K'tonton.
          Stories from her: The adventures of K'tonton, K'tonton in Israel, and from K'tonton on
an island in the sea.
          SUMMARY: The adventures of a thumb-sized boy born into a Jewish family.   1.
Children's
stories, American [1. Jews—fiction] I. Hirsch, Marilyn. II. Title. PZ7.W435Be [Fic] 80-20177
ISBN 0-8276-0184-0   ISBN 0-8276-0187-5 (pbk.)

In grateful remembrance of those who, fifty years ago,
set K'tonton on his path,
and to each friend, child and grownup
who has helped him on his way.—S.R.W.

Contents

Introduction
Francine Klagsbrun

HEN I first met K'tonton he was artfully dodging a chopping knife. I held my breath as I watched him slip and slide around a bowl of raw fish while that ominous knife moved steadily up and down.

Watched him? Well, not really, I suppose. I was in a classroom—perhaps first or second grade—and a teacher was reading aloud from the adventures of the little thumbkin.

"Ketchoo!" sneezed K'tonton. "Ketchoo!"

Up to his nose went his hands and down into the bowl of fish went K'tonton. Ugh, how sticky it was! But the stickiness was the least of his troubles.

I sat at a desk and K'tonton existed only on the pages of a book, but I saw him as clearly—more clearly—than I saw the teacher. I saw him struggling through that mess of fish as the chopping knife (the exact knife my mother used for chopping liver) drew ever closer. I heard him cry for help, then watched as two adult fingers lifted him gingerly out of the bowl. With him, I felt the relief of cool faucet water rinsing away the sticky fish.

That image of K'tonton was stamped on my memory. There were other books and other characters, of course, that filled my childhood fantasies, but K'tonton's place was unique. It is not simply nostalgia that holds me in rapt attention as I reread every word of the stories in this collection, not simply gilded recollections of childhood that fill me with warmth as I retrace the escapades of that tiny fellow. It's something more, something about K'tonton himself.

"Why do you enjoy K'tonton stories?" I ask my ten-year-old daughter, whose reading encompasses far more sophisticated modern fiction.

"He's so cute," she answers. "And I like his adventures. You feel as though you're him, and all those things are happening to you."

Ah, there's the heart of it. Cute little K'tonton is the child in all of us, the mischief-maker who somehow outsmarts the serious grownup world to which we're supposed to conform. Yet there's nothing threatening about K'tonton's activities. Whether he's swinging on a *lulav* or hiding away in a suitcase bound for Israel, his "misbehavior" is always rooted in a deep love for family and tradition. We—children and adults—can enjoy his antics because in the end they reaffirm the things we believe in most strongly.

And then, K'tonton has a conscience, a pressing sense of right and wrong that adds poignancy to so many of his experiences. He *knows* he wronged the kitten, and no one but he can right that wrong, no matter how long he fasts on Yom Kippur. Cynics may mock the naiveté of our hero's moral absolutes, but children understand such absolutes, children govern their lives by them.

K'tonton's special combination of mischief and morality, of Jewish observance and universal values, set him apart from other children's literature characters from his very beginnings. Those beginnings go back to September 1930, when K'tonton made his debut in the first issue of the Women's League *Outlook*, the journal of the national organization of sisterhoods of the Conservative movement. The opening pages of the journal proudly bore New Year's greetings from Mrs. Cyrus Adler, Mrs. Louis Ginzberg, Mrs. M. M. Kaplan, Mrs. Alexander Marx, and other luminaries of the Women's League. Discreetly sprinkled among its columns were advertisements for such items as "Four little volumes" of stories for children, "nicely boxed" at $1.00 a set, and "Victrola records" of *seder* melodies going at $1.25 a set of two. And tucked away on page eleven, in the "Children's Corner," was the tale of a loving couple who wanted a child so badly they wouldn't care, said the wife, "if he were no bigger than a thumb." Their wish came true, and K'tonton entered our world.

K'tonton's adventures so intrigued young readers of *Outlook*, and older ones as well, that his stories graced many subsequent issues. They were gathered into the first collection of K'tonton tales, *The Adventures of K'tonton*, published by the Women's League in 1935, and revised in 1964. Two other collections of K'tonton lore appeared later: *K'tonton in Israel*, in 1964; and *K'tonton on an Island in the Sea*, in 1976. All are represented in this collection.

The success of her little character never surprised his creator, Sadie Rose Weilerstein, the "Mrs. W." who sometimes records K'tonton's actions in the stories. She had already established herself as a children's writer with *What Danny Did*, her first book of stories built around Jewish themes. She knew her tiny new hero well, knew just how to balance his precocity with childhood curiosity, his daring with dependency. She also knew her audience. As the introduction to *The Adventures of K'tonton* says, "His dreams and ambitions, the festivals he celebrates, the ceremonies he delights in, are shared in varying degrees by Jewish children everywhere."

The Victrola records advertised in the first issue of *Outlook* no longer exist, and one would be hard put to find a set of four boxed books for $1.00 today. But K'tonton goes on, charming another generation of children, sparking in their parents the glow of remembered satisfactions.

"I guess size isn't everything," says K'tonton at the end of the last story in this collection.

K'tonton's size, appealing as it is, is only part of his attraction. The rest is Sadie Rose Weilerstein's magic.

The Best of K'tonton

K'tonton arrives

NCE upon a time there lived a husband and a wife. They had everything in the world to make them happy, or almost everything: a good snug house, clothes to keep them warm, white bread, wine and fish for Friday night, and a special pudding—a *kugel*—every Sabbath. Only one thing was missing and that was a child.

"Ah," the woman would sigh, "if only I could have a child! I shouldn't mind if he were no bigger than a thumb."

One day—it was on Sukkot, the Feast of Tabernacles—she was praying in the synagogue, when she happened to look down. There at her side stood a little old woman. Such a strange, wrinkled old woman with deep, kind eyes peering up at her from under a shawl!

"Why do you look so sad," asked the old woman, "and why do you pray so earnestly?"

"I am sad," answered the wife, "because I have no child.

Ah, that I might have a child! I shouldn't mind if he were no bigger than a thumb."

"In that case," said the little old woman, "I shall tell you what to do. Has your husband an *etrog?*"

"Indeed he has," said the wife, "an *etrog*, a *mehudar*." (That means that it was a very fine *etrog*, a perfect, sweet-smelling one, a citron that had come all the way from Israel.)

"Then," said the old woman, "on the last day of Sukkot you must take the *etrog* and bite off the end, and you shall have your wish."

The wife thanked the little old woman kindly. When the last day of Sukkot came, she bit off the end of the *etrog* just as she had been told. Sure enough, before the year had passed a little baby was born to her. It was a dear little boy baby, with black eyes and black hair, dimples in his knees, and thumbs just right for sucking. There was only one thing odd about him. He was exactly the size of a thumb, not one bit smaller or larger.

The wife laughed when she saw him. I don't know whether she laughed because she was so glad, or because it seemed so funny to have a baby as big as a thumb. Whichever it was, the husband said, "We shall call him Isaac, because Isaac in Hebrew means laughter." Then, because they were so thankful to God for sending him, they gave the baby a second name, Samuel. But, of course, they couldn't call such a little baby, a baby no bigger than a thumb, Isaac Samuel all the time. So for every day they called him K'tonton, which means very, very little; and that's exactly what he was.

The first thing they had to do was to find a cradle for the baby to sleep in.

"Fetch me the *etrog* box," the wife said to her husband. "It was the *etrog* that brought my precious K'tonton and the *etrog* box shall be his cradle."

She lifted the cover of the box, a curving, rounded cover. When she turned it over it rocked gently to and fro. Then she

took the flax that the *etrog* had been wrapped in, and spun it and wove it into softest linen. Out of the linen she made a coverlet and sheet. Wherever she went and whatever she did, little K'tonton in his little cradle went with her. When she kneaded the dough for the Sabbath, she set the cradle on the table beside her.

"It will put a blessing in the bread," she said.

Often she placed the cradle in an eastern window. "Perhaps a sunbeam from Israel will steal down to him."

She fed him milk with honey in it—Israeli honey. "The Torah is like milk and honey," she said. "I will feed you milk and honey now, and when you grow older you will feed on Torah."

Sometimes K'tonton opened his tiny mouth and cried. You would never believe so loud a sound could come from so small a mouth. Then K'tonton's mother carried him, cradle and all, into the room where his father sat studying all day long in the big books of the Talmud. Back and forth K'tonton's father swayed reciting the Hebrew page. Back and forth K'tonton rocked in his cradle listening to the words and thinking them the pleasantest sound he had ever heard, even pleasanter than his mother's lullabies.

So K'tonton grew until he was as tall as his father's middle finger. By this time he wasn't a baby any longer. He was three years old, and wore trousers and a little shirt and a tiny *arba kanfot* of finest silk. You could see the fringes of the *arba kanfot* sticking out from under his shirt.

Now, when K'tonton's mother was cooking and baking for the Sabbath, there was no cooing baby to watch her from his cradle. No—there was a busy little chatterbox of a K'tonton, dancing about on the table, peeping into the cinnamon box, hiding behind the sugar bowl, asking a question, so many questions, that at last his mother would say, "Blessings on your little head, K'tonton. If you don't let me keep my mind on my work, I'll be putting salt in the cake and sugar in the fish." But before anything of the sort happened, K'tonton had a most exciting adventure. Only that is a story in itself.

K'tonton takes a ride on a chopping knife and wishes he hadn't

T was Friday and K'tonton sat cross-legged on the kitchen table, watching his mother chop the fish for the Sabbath. Up and down, up and down went the chopping knife in the wooden bowl, chip, chop, chip, chop!

Now if there was one thing K'tonton loved it was a ride.

"If I could just reach that chopping knife," he thought, "I could sit down in the center of it with a leg on each side. It would be like riding horseback."

"Tap! Tap!" came a sound at the door. K'tonton's mother put down the knife. "Sit still until I get back, K'tonton. Don't get into mischief," she called as she went off to see who was knocking.

But K'tonton was too busy looking about him to hear her. How could he reach the top of that chopping bowl? Ah, there was a bag of sugar tied with a string! In a moment K'tonton had taken hold of the string and was climbing up, up to the very top. Then he sprang lightly to the wooden bowl, slid down the inner side and landed right in the center of the chopping knife. Just as he seated himself astride the blade, his mother returned. A neighbor's wife was with her. They were so busy talking that K'tonton's mother picked up the knife and began chopping away without even noticing that her little son was on it.

Up and down, up and down went the chopping knife, chip, chop, chip, chop! Up and down went K'tonton, holding fast to the blade.

"Gee-ap!" he shouted. "Gee-ap!" But the chop-chop of the knife was so loud, his mother didn't hear him.

"This is a good ride! This is a jolly ride," thought K'tonton, bouncing up and down. "Why didn't I think of it before?" Suddenly, down on his head came a shower of pepper.

"Ketchoo!" sneezed K'tonton. "Ketchoo!"

Up to his nose went his hands and down into the bowl of fish went K'tonton. Ugh, how sticky it was! But the stickiness was the least of his troubles. Up and down, up and down the knife was going; and up and down and in and out jumped K'tonton, dodging the sharp blade.

"Help! Help!" he called, but his mother was still talking to the neighbor and didn't hear him.

"This is the end of me," thought K'tonton. "I know that Jonah was saved from the inside of a fish, but I never heard of anyone being saved from a bowl of chopped fish."

He was all covered with fish by this time. His legs were so tired he could hardly jump any more.

"I'd better say my *Shema,*" said K'tonton.

But at that moment the chopping knife was lifted out of the bowl and K'tonton's mother was looking down into it.

"Ugh! There's a fly in the fish."

Down into the bowl went her spoon and up came K'tonton! Such a sputtering, struggling, sorry looking K'tonton!

"K'tonton!" cried his mother, "what have you been doing to yourself?"

"Taking a ride, Mother, a ride on the chopping knife."

"A ride? A ride on the chopping knife? God be thanked who preserves the simple!"

Then she picked K'tonton up in her two fingers, and held him under the faucet until there wasn't a bit of sticky fish left.

You may be sure K'tonton never rode on a chopping knife again.

21

K'TONTON TAKES A RIDE
ON A CHOPPING KNIFE
AND WISHES HE HADN'T

K'tonton goes to synagogue and swings on a *lulav*

WOULD you like to hear how K'tonton went to synagogue for the first time? It was on Sukkot. Father had placed the *etrog* carefully into its box, ready to be carried to the synagogue.

"May I go with you, Father?" K'tonton asked.

"Wait until you're a little bigger," said Father. "Next year will be time enough."

But K'tonton did not want to wait until next year. He wanted to go now, this very day. What do you suppose he did? When Father wasn't looking, he climbed inside the *etrog* box and hid beneath the flax.

Soon the box was lifted. It was being carried through the streets. Now they were in the synagogue. K'tonton could tell by the sound of the prayers. For a while he sat listening to the voice of the cantor. Then he rose cautiously on tiptoe, pushed up the cover of the box and peeked out. There wasn't a thing he

could see! A high wooden bench rose like a wall before him.

"I'll have to get up higher," thought K'tonton.

He looked about for something tall that he might climb. Ah! there was a *lulav*, a palm branch, leaning against the bench. It rose up straight, and green, and tall. K'tonton grasped it with both hands and began climbing. It was easy at first. The braided holder supported his feet. But once he had passed the willow and the myrtle twigs, climbing became hard and slippery. Up, up he went, holding fast to the branch, higher than the bench tops, higher than the heads of the people.

Now at last he could see the synagogue. How beautiful it was! He had never dreamed a place could be so large. And so many men all wrapped in their *tallitim*, their long fringed prayer shawls.

But most beautiful of all was the *aron kodesh*, the Holy Ark. On its crimson curtains, flowers were embroidered and pomegranates and golden lions. K'tonton knew that behind those curtains were the *Sifrei Torah*, the scrolls of the holy law. His heart filled with awe just to think of it.

Suddenly the *lulav*, to which K'tonton clung, shook and rose into the air! What had happened? K'tonton held on tight to keep from tumbling, and looked down.

His father had risen and taken the *lulav* in his hand. All about rose other *lulavim*. The synagogue was like a forest of palm branches. They trembled and swayed; and K'tonton, clinging tightly to his father's *lulav*, swayed with them.

Oh, what a swinging and a swaying that was! East and west, north and south, up toward heaven, down toward earth!

"Hodu l'Adonai ki tov," sang the people. "Praise the Lord for He is good."

Again the branches swayed. East and west, north and south, up toward heaven, down toward earth. K'tonton, swinging on the *lulav*, forgot that he had run away, forgot that he was supposed to be hiding. *"Hodu l'Adonai ki tov!"* he sang. His shrill high treble rose above the voices of the people.

In a moment every eye in the synagogue was on him. Men whispered and pointed. Women in the gallery crowded close to the railing. Even the cantor looked straight toward him. As for K'tonton's father, he gasped in astonishment.

"K'tonton, you might have fallen and been hurt!" he cried as he snatched the little fellow from the *lulav*. "How do you come to be here at all?"

Soberly K'tonton told the story of his adventure.

"If I were a proper parent, I would spank you," said his father; but K'tonton could see by the twinkle in his eye that the rod would be spared. So K'tonton stayed in the synagogue to join in the *Hoshanot* prayers, and march in the procession of the palms.

Up in the gallery a little old woman smiled and nodded, a wrinkled little woman with deep, kind eyes peering out from under a shawl.

"A wonder child," she murmured. "Even when he runs away, where does he run to? The synagogue!"

K'tonton takes a ride on a runaway *dreidel*

T was Hanukkah, the Feast of Lights. The first little Hanukkah light was shining in the window. Aunt Gittel and Uncle Israel had come to visit. So had the little old *Bobbe*. You remember her, don't you? The little old woman who sat next to K'tonton's mother in synagogue and told her what to do if she wanted to have a child! From the kitchen came the pleasant sizzle, sizzle of frying *latkes*. Everyone was laughing and singing and chattering, everyone but K'tonton. K'tonton sat in a corner by himself as sober as a weekday. There wasn't a smile on his face, not the tiniest bit of a smile. And all because of his great ambition. He had told the lions on the Hanukkah *menorah* all about that ambition the day before.

"See my *tzedakah* box—the blue one with the white star. It's where I put my charity. I'm going to fill it to the very top. Clinkety, clink, away the pennies will go to Israel! They're to buy land, you know—for the Jewish farmers there, the *halutzim*.

26
K'TONTON TAKES
A RIDE ON A
RUNAWAY DREIDEL

They ought to get a good piece of land with a whole box full of money."

But, of course, if K'tonton wanted to fill his box, he had to have Hanukkah *gelt,* coins given to children for Hanukkah. But no one in the room had offered him any, not Father, not Mother, not *Bobbe,* not Uncle Israel or Aunt Gittel.

"Maybe they're hungry and that makes them forget," thought K'tonton. "Perhaps they'll remember after they've had their *latkes.*" But no! Mother brought the *latkes* in, a great plateful of potato pancakes for the grownups, a tiny plateful for K'tonton. Every *latke* was eaten and still no one said a word about Hanukkah *gelt.*

"Perhaps I should remind them," thought K'tonton. "I'll go right up and I'll say, 'Don't you know it's Hanukkah? Don't you know you're supposed to give Hanukkah *gelt* on Hanukkah?'"

But no. It wouldn't be polite to ask for Hanukkah *gelt.*

"Come here, my little sober one," called Uncle Israel picking K'tonton up in his hand. "Where's your Hanukkah smile? Get the *dreidel,* Gittel! We've got to wake our K'tonton up."

Out came the *dreidel,* the whirling Hanukkah top with Hebrew letters on the sides. Uncle Israel seated K'tonton on it. Whirl! Twirl! and K'tonton and the Hanukkah *dreidel* were spinning about on the table. Round and round, round and round whirled the *dreidel.* Faster and faster, faster and faster, faster and faster! Then slower and slower and slower! It swayed. It stopped. K'tonton peered over the side.

"*Gimel!*" he called. His cheeks were rosy with excitement. He had forgotten his disappointment, or almost forgotten it.

"Your turn, Aunt Gittel!" he called.

Whirl, twirl! The *dreidel* was off again. Straight across the table it went with K'tonton on it.

"Watch out!" cried Father. "It's going over the side."

And over the side it went. Down from the table, across the floor, out through the doorway! Spin, bump! Spin, bump! Down

the stairs and out into the street! Down the stairs and out into the street after the runaway *dreidel* went Father! And after Father, Mother, and after Mother, Uncle Israel and *Bobbe* and Aunt Gittel.

"Stop the *dreidel!* Stop it! Stop it!" called Father to a fat policeman at the corner.

"Stop it! Please stop it!" called Mother, who was almost in tears.

"Stop it! Stop the *dreidel!*" cried *Bobbe* and Aunt Gittel and Uncle Israel all together.

But the policeman didn't know what a *dreidel* was.

On and on sped the Hanukkah top with K'tonton holding fast. He laughed aloud. He was enjoying the ride. Now they were at the corner. Now they had turned the corner and were spinning on—down a dark alley, around another corner, on and on and on. And still the *dreidel* spun. Would it ever stop? K'tonton was not laughing now. Perhaps this was a punishment. Hadn't he sulked about the Hanukkah *gelt?* Hadn't he spoiled the joy of the holiday with his frown? He must accept whatever befell him.

"*Gam zu l'tovah,*" said K'tonton. "This, too, is for the best!"

As he spoke the *dreidel* swerved. It turned into a gutter. It swayed drunkenly. It stopped. K'tonton sprang to his feet and looked about. Something was gleaming in the darkness. It wasn't—it couldn't be—but it was! A big round shining quarter!

Up came Father panting and out of breath. He stooped over the gutter to pick up his frightened K'tonton. But K'tonton wasn't frightened. He was laughing and hugging a shining quarter to his breast.

"Hanukkah *gelt*, Father!" cried K'tonton, "For my *tzedakah* box."

"Hanukkah *gelt?*" said Father. I forgot all about Hanukkah *gelt!*"

Up came Mother with her handkerchief ready to wipe away

K'tonton's tears. But there were no tears to wipe away.

"Hanukkah *gelt?*" said Mother. "I forgot all about Hanukkah *gelt!*"

Up came Uncle Israel and Aunt Gittel and the little old *Bobbe*. "Hanukkah *gelt,* Uncle Israel! See my Hanukkah *gelt, Bobbe,* Aunt Gittel!" And K'tonton held his precious quarter high.

"Hanukkah *gelt!*" cried Bobbe and Aunt Gittel and Uncle Israel together. "To think we forgot all about Hanukkah *gelt!*"

Then Father picked up his little son and carried him home, *dreidel,* Hanukkah *gelt,* and all, down the street, up the stairs into the house, straight to the big blue and white *tzedakah* box. High up to the top of the box K'tonton was lifted. And then . . . and then . . .

Father emptied his pockets. He emptied every penny, nickel, quarter, and dime that was in them. And Uncle Israel emptied his pockets. And Mother and Aunt Gittel emptied their pocketbooks. And little old *Bobbe* took out her handkerchief and untied the knot in a corner and shook out eight shining new pennies, one for each night of the holiday. The Hanukkah *gelt* was piled up at the side of the blue box so high it covered the star. Father handed up the coins and K'tonton rolled up his sleeves and pushed each one down the slot of the *tzedakah* box.

"Hurrah!" cried K'tonton as the last Hanukkah coin went clinkety, clink, clink into the box. "Hurray for Hanukkah *gelt!* Hurray for *Eretz Yisrael!* Hurray for the runaway *dreidel.*"

K'tonton masquerades on Purim

ATHER," said K'tonton, "when you were a little boy, did you dress up on Purim and wear a mask?"

"What a question!"

"And did you go to other people's houses and sing songs?"

"Of course!"

"Could I dress up and masquerade?"

"A little fellow like you, K'tonton? You would be left behind under a doormat. But I'll make you a *grogger*. That will be better than masquerading." K'tonton's father took out a penknife and a bit of wood and made him a beautiful noise-making *grogger*.

"Ras! Ras! Ras!" went the *grogger* as K'tonton whirled it about.

"It's nice to have a *grogger*," said K'tonton, "but not so nice as masquerading on Purim. I'd better talk to Mother."

Mother was in the kitchen rolling out *imberlach*, ginger candy sticks. She lifted K'tonton to the table.

"Could I masquerade on Purim?" asked K'tonton.

"You?" said Mother. "Listen to the child! Haven't I lost you enough times already? But I'll tell you what I'll do. I'll make you a little *hamantash* all for yourself. See! I've been pounding the poppy seeds." She pointed to a brass mortar on the table.

"Oh," said K'tonton, "poppy seed with honey?"

"Honey of course," said Mother. "What else? Now sit still, K'tonton. I'll be back in a minute."

Off Mother went. K'tonton crossed his legs and waited.

"A minute is a long time," he said after a while.

He sat still again.

"I guess it must be two minutes. I guess it must be nine minutes. I guess I'll just get up and take a look at that poppy seed."

Up the side of a sack of flour he ran. Now he could see deep down into the mortar. He could see the pounder leaning against the side.

"That's a good slide," said K'tonton. He loved sliding down things. "I'll slide down and take a taste of that poppy seed. Mother wouldn't mind if I just took a little taste."

The next moment his legs were over the top of the pounder and he was sliding down. A thought popped into his head. "I must stop before I reach the bottom. I might get stuck." But he couldn't stop. He was going too fast. Blimp! He was in poppy seed up to his waist.

And there was Mother's voice coming toward him. "Where's that K'tonton? I can't seem to keep track of him today. Well, I'll have to make the *hamantashen* without him."

K'tonton felt the mortar lifted and turned over. The next moment he was tumbling head over heels into a big bowl with poppy seed all around him. You couldn't tell which was poppy seed and which was K'tonton.

"Mother! Mother!" K'tonton began, but a stream of honey

was flowing over him. The words caught in the honey and stuck fast.

And now a big wooden spoon came down into the bowl. It picked K'tonton up. It tossed him! It chased him! Round and round went K'tonton with the wooden spoon close behind. It caught him at last. It lifted him up into the air. It set him down in the middle of something soft. Dough! a flat piece of dough! K'tonton was being made into a *hamantash!*

"I must speak! I must call!" thought K'tonton. "My voice! Where is my voice?" It was gone. By the time it returned, he had been slipped into a pan and was being carried off.

A *hamantash!* That meant he would be put into an oven, a fiery furnace like Abraham and Daniel's companions. And God would not save him as He had saved Daniel's companions and Abraham. Had he not disobeyed his dear mother?

"Dear God," K'tonton prayed, "save me from the fiery oven even if I don't deserve it."

A voice was speaking. K'tonton pressed his ear to the hole in the *hamantash* and listened.

"I'll leave the cakes on the shelf here to rise." The pan was lifted. Then all was still.

Then he wasn't to be put into the oven, not for a little while at least. He might yet escape. But how? He tried to move. His arms were stuck fast to his sides.

"I'll eat my way out," K'tonton said. He ate and he ate and he ate. He ate so much he felt he could never look at honey or a poppy seed again. The hole grew bigger and bigger. It grew so big he could stick his head out. He could wriggle his hands loose. His arms and his legs were out. He was free.

Far, far below was the table. K'tonton shut his eyes tight and jumped—safe into the middle of the sack of flour.

But his troubles were not yet over.

Creak, creak, came a step across the floor.

"Mother!" thought K'tonton. "I must hide until I get this poppy seed washed off."

He slipped into a plate and hid behind a pile of *imberlach*.

Mother's voice came nearer. "Father," it said, "I'm going to take some Purim cakes and fruit—*shalach manot*—to the new little boy next door. He has been sick in bed ever since they moved in. Poor little fellow! The sweets may cheer him up a bit."

She threw a napkin over the plate.

"Look after K'tonton, Father," she said. "He's somewhere about."

She lifted the plate and was off. And there was K'tonton in the *shalach manot* dish with cakes and candies and *haman-tashen* all about him.

"I wonder what is going to happen next?" he thought.

He was so tired he snuggled down at the bottom of the dish and shut his eyes. In another minute he was asleep.

"What has happened? Where am I?" said K'tonton when he opened his eyes a little later.

He peered cautiously over the side of a *hamantash* and looked about. He was in a strange room. The dish was lying on a table near a bed, and on the bed lay a young boy propped up with pillows. Such a pale, unhappy-looking little fellow! He was staring soberly at the *shalach manot*, at the cakes, the Purim candies, the *hamantashen*, but he did not taste a thing and there wasn't a smile on his face. Something hurt inside of K'tonton.

"One oughtn't to look like that on Purim," he thought. "Purim is a good day, a day of gladness and feasting, a day of sending gifts to one another. The *Megillah* says so."

K'tonton forgot that he was supposed to be hiding. He forgot he was covered with poppy seed. He forgot that he was dusted with flour. He knew only that he had to make that little boy smile. He stepped from behind the *hamantash* and bowed low.

The boy's mouth opened and his eyes grew as big as saucers.

"The inside of a *hamantash* came alive!"

He stared hard.

"It must be a toy," he decided. "I suppose there are springs inside." He reached out his hand to feel, but K'tonton sprang back.

"I'm not a toy," he said. "I'm not the inside of a *hamantash*—though I was inside one," he added truthfully. "I . . . I . . ." It was then that the great thought dawned on him. "I'm a Purim masquerader and I'm dressed up in poppy seed and I've come to other people's houses, to your house, to sing Purim songs."

At that he lifted his shrill voice and began to sing:

Happy, happy Purim,
Happy Purim day!

For a minute the boy sat perfectly still and stared. Then he threw back his head and laughed. Such a happy, jolly, hearty, rollicking laugh, a regular Purim laugh! Ha, ha, ha, ha, ha! Ho, ho, ho, he, he!

"What could have happened?" cried the little boy's mother, who was in the next room. "I haven't heard David laugh in weeks."

She hurried into the bedroom and K'tonton's mother followed her. There was David laughing and clapping his hands; and there in the middle of the *shalach manot* dish, black with poppy seed and dusted with flour, was a tiny little fellow singing and dancing away.

"K'tonton!" cried his mother. "How did you get here? What does this mean?"

"I'm . . . I'm the inside of a *hamantash*," said K'tonton. "I'm in someone else's house. I'm masquerading as you did when you were a little girl."

"Please let him stay, please," begged David. "We're having such a good time."

K'tonton's mother hurried home and fetched him a clean little suit and shirt. When she came back she scrubbed K'tonton and dressed him in his holiday clothes.

K'tonton's father came too. He brought a *Megillah* with him, the special scroll that tells the whole story of Purim, all about the King and Mordecai and the wicked Haman, and how good Queen Esther saved the Jews. K'tonton's father chanted the *Megillah*, and K'tonton ran along under the words—to keep the place—and every time he came to the name of the wicked Haman he whirled his *grogger*. Ras! Ras! Ras!

Then they sang songs and ate the cakes and *imberlach* and *hamantashen*, and everyone had such a good time. No one thought of scolding K'tonton at all.

K'tonton is forgiven on Yom Kippur

T all began the day after Rosh Hashanah, the Jewish New Year. K'tonton and his Mother were in the kitchen.

Meow, meow! came a faint sound.

A thin little gray and white kitten stood in the doorway. No one knew whose kitten it was or where it had come from. K'tonton didn't know. His father didn't know. His mother didn't know! It looked at K'tonton and mewed plaintively.

"It's hungry," said K'tonton. "Give it some milk, please, Mother."

But Mother shook her head.

"If I give it milk, it will be back every day."

Just the same, she filled a saucer with milk and set it down in the doorway.

Lap, lap, lap! In and out, in and out went the kitten's pink tongue until the saucer was empty.

Next day the kitten came back just as Mother had said it would. On the third day it came too. Mother was busy making *taiglach*, honey pastries. She set a cup of honey at the edge of the table and fetched the kitten its dish of milk. Father called her at that moment.

In and out, in and out went the kitten's pink tongue. K'tonton watched her from his place on the table. Perhaps it made him hungry to see her lap the milk so greedily, but his eyes turned to a trickle of honey running down the side of the cup. He stuck his finger into the golden trickle and licked it off. M-m-m! It was good. And there was more honey around the rim of the cup. K'tonton leaned forward to reach it, when crash! down went the cup from the table. The honey ran in a stream across the floor. The startled kitten sprang up and ran through the stream of honey to the door.

Just then in came Mother.

"Oh, oh!" she cried, "in my honey! And it's all I have in the house. K'tonton, did you do this?"

K'tonton said nothing.

Mother's eyes fell on the kitten's sticky little footprints.

"It's that kitten," she said. "It must have sprung on the table and upset the cup. I told you I should never have given it milk."

She looked sternly at K'tonton as if she suspected him of shielding the kitten.

K'tonton's heart beat wildly.

"Speak up, K'tonton," something was whispering inside him. "Tell Mother you upset the cup. Don't let the poor kitten be blamed."

But K'tonton did not speak up. He just stood there hanging his head.

Next day when the kitten came for its milk, Mother shooed it away.

"Scat!" she said. "Scat! I'll have no more mischief."

Oh, how guilty K'tonton felt! But by that time it was even harder to explain than the day before.

Soon it would be Yom Kippur, the Day of Judgment, and K'tonton had this sin on his heart.

"Even the fish in the sea tremble on Yom Kippur," thought K'tonton. "How much more should I be trembling."

"I'll give all my pennies for charity," he said. "I won't keep even one. I'll fast all day and I'll pray. God will know I am sorry. No one could be more sorry than I."

He was thinking of the verse in the prayer book, "Charity, prayer, and penitence avert the evil decree."

But there was something else that the Torah taught, which K'tonton was trying hard not to think about.

"If a man wrong his neighbor, let him go to his neighbor and make right the wrong. Otherwise Yom Kippur cannot atone for him."

K'tonton pushed the thought aside.

At *Minhah*—the afternoon service—he dropped a coin in every saucer that had been set out in the doorway of the synagogue; a coin for Israel, for the *yeshivot,* one for the aged, one for the orphans, one for the hungry.

"The kitten is hungry without its milk," the voice inside K'tonton whispered. "Maybe it's an orphan, too."

K'tonton put the thought aside.

Next morning he refused the milk which Mother offered him.

"I'm fasting," he said, and went off to the synagogue with his father.

All through the morning K'tonton stood on the arm of Father's bench and prayed with the congregation. He swayed, he joined in the responses; he beat his breast at each verse of the confession. When they came to the part, "For the sin which

I have committed before Thee in wronging a neighbor," he beat it especially hard.

The morning service was over.

"Go home now and eat, K'tonton," Father said. "See, your friend Sammy has eaten and he is older than you."

K'tonton shook his head.

The *Musaf* service was over. Mother sent down a message. "Send K'tonton home at once. The child will be ill if he fasts any longer. David will take him. I have left his dinner on the table."

"Come on, K'tonton," urged his other friend David.

K'tonton was tempted. He thought of the fresh *hallah,* of the little fish ball that Mother had made especially for him, of the good milk. But the thought of milk brought the kitten to mind. Because of his sin the poor kitten had no milk.

"Please, please, Father, let me fast. I must!" begged K'tonton.

He spoke so earnestly, Father had not the heart to insist.

On and on went the service. David had gone home to eat and had returned. K'tonton felt odd and shaky. So this was what it was like to be hungry! Maybe this was how the kitten felt.

Maybe it was standing in the doorway now, all weak and empty. K'tonton could hear its plaintive *meow.* He raised his voice higher in prayer, but the voice inside whispered.

"Foolish K'tonton, what if you don't have your milk? That won't give the kitten *its* milk. Go and tell the truth to your mother."

K'tonton could stand it no longer. He clutched the fringe of Father's *tallit.*

"Father, Father," he called. "Take me to Mother. I must go to Mother at once."

Father looked down, startled. "K'tonton, little son, what is wrong? Are you sick?"

"No, no," said K'tonton, and he sobbed out the whole story!

In the shadows of the Yom Kippur afternoon, K'tonton and David stood in the kitchen watching a thin gray and white kitten lapping up its milk. In and out, in and out went the little pink tongue.

"Kitten, will you forgive me?" asked K'tonton soberly.

Meow, meow! said the kitten.

K'tonton knew he was forgiven.

K'tonton goes out into the wide world

'TONTON sat in the synagogue in his own little seat. It was set high on the back of his father's bench, a tiny seat just the size for a K'tonton as big as a thumb. But he wasn't praying. He was thinking—thinking about wishes.

How did K'tonton come to be thinking about wishes in a synagogue? It was on account of the prayers for the new month of Iyar, which comes in the spring.

"May the wishes of our hearts be fulfilled for good," K'tonton's father prayed.

"May the wishes of our hearts be fulfilled," K'tonton prayed—but he didn't add "for good." Instead he began thinking about wishes.

There were so many wishes in K'tonton's heart. He wished that he could go out into the world to see God's wonders: falling stars, lofty mountains, deserts, the great sea. He wished he could sail across the sea. He wished he could fly in the air.

"Father," he whispered, "I have never said the blessing over the great sea." This was K'tonton's way of saying that he had never seen the ocean.

"Haven't you?" replied his father, and went on praying.

K'tonton tried again when services were over.

"Lag b'Omer will be here in three weeks, Father," he said. Lag b'Omer is the scholars' holiday when Hebrew-school boys and girls go on a picnic. "*Must* a Lag b'Omer picnic be in the woods? Couldn't it be at the seashore?"

"So that's what has been on your mind," K'tonton's father said with a smile. "A picnic at the seashore! Well, perhaps it can be managed."

And it *was* managed.

On Lag b'Omer afternoon K'tonton stood on his father's shoulder, looking out over the ocean. His mother stood beside them. The sea stretched out and out. Waves rolled in like watery mountains. K'tonton lifted his voice joyfully:

Blessed art Thou, O Lord our God, King of the universe, who has made the great sea.

All afternoon K'tonton explored the wonders of the beach. He played hide-and-seek among the seashells. He slid down stacks of seaweed. He ate the tiny sandwiches tucked into his coat pocket. Father and Mother had their own sandwiches. All of K'tonton's put together would not have made one good mouthful for them.

"It's growing windy," Mother said at last. "We'd better start for home."

She stuck K'tonton into his father's hatband, and they set off briskly along the boardwalk. What a grand view K'tonton had high up on his father's hat. He saw great gulls wheeling overhead. He saw an old gull pulling at a clamshell on the beach below. He saw an island in the distance.

The wind grew stronger. It lifted the waves and whipped them into froth.

"Look, Father," K'tonton called excitedly through the roaring of the sea. "It's just like the psalm says: 'He commanded and raised the stormy wind. It lifted up the waves thereof.' "

As he spoke a gust of wind lifted something that wasn't a wave. It was the hat from K'tonton's father's head.

Away went the hat with K'tonton on it. After the hat went K'tonton's frantic father and mother. Before they could catch it, it flew over the railing and alighted–right on the head of the old seagull.

Awk! Awk! screamed the gull, trying to shake the strange burden from its head.

K'tonton laughed out loud. A gull with a hat on was so funny. But he stopped, ashamed. "I'm laughing at a creature in distress," he thought.

The next minute K'tonton himself was in distress. The frightened gull flapped its wings, rose into the air, and flew out over the sea.

"I'm flying like a bird," K'tonton said to himself in astonishment. "The wishes of my heart are being fulfilled." But he didn't say it happily. He knew now why his father was so careful to add "for good" when he prayed.

Again a gust of wind lifted the hat—this time off the head of the gull. Down went the hat, spinning through the air, around and down, around and down, with K'tonton still in the hatband.

And now another wish of K'tonton's heart was being fulfilled, though he wished it weren't. He was sailing on the sea, with his father's hat for a boat. How great the sea seemed! Up went a wave, and up went K'tonton on his father's hat. Down went the wave, and down went the hat and K'tonton. Up, down, up, down!

"I'm going to be sick," thought K'tonton, "—unless I drown," he added as a wave went over him. The wave drenched his shoes and the new Passover suit his mother had made him. K'tonton held tight to the hatband and began reciting psalms:

All Thy waves and Thy billows have gone over me.
Save me, O my God, save me.

As he spoke, the hat whirled around three times and began floating toward shore. But not the shore where K'tonton had left his parents. It was the shore of the island K'tonton had seen in the distance!

The wind died down. The waves grew quiet. Closer and closer to the shore floated the hat, with K'tonton on it. It stopped at last, caught among the reeds along the shore.

For the moment, K'tonton was safe. But he wasn't home. "Next time," K'tonton thought, "when I pray that my wishes be fulfilled, I'll add 'for good.' But right now I must learn to live with God's creatures."

Sabbath on the island

I T was Friday. *Shabbat*, the Sabbath, the day of rest and joy, would begin at sundown. But K'tonton looked anything but joyful. He thought of his mother. Friday was her busiest day. She cooked and baked *hallah*, the Sabbath bread. She cleaned the house. She polished the candlesticks.

"There," she would say when the house was filled with good smells, with the family dressed in their Sabbath clothes, the table set with wine and *hallahs*, when the candles were waiting to be lit. "Now we're ready for the Sabbath Queen."

"What kind of *Shabbat* will the Queen find when she comes to this island?" K'tonton asked himself sadly. No *hallah*, no wine for *Kiddush*. Not even *Shabbat* lights!"

K'tonton was sitting with his hands in his lap, thinking about his troubles, when a saying of the rabbis came into his mind: "You are not obliged to finish the task, but neither are you excused from beginning it."

K'tonton jumped up.

"Alone on an island I can't do everything we're supposed to do for *Shabbat*, but I'll do what I can," he resolved.

Now K'tonton became as busy as his mother was on Fridays. First he took off his only shirt, washed it, and hung it on the stiff grasses to dry. Next he made a tiny broom out of twigs and gave the floor of his house a good sweeping. (His house was a large brown shell. The front of it looked something like a horseshoe with a domed roof over it. The back end had a long, bony tail.) Then K'tonton sprinkled the floor with clean sand.

"I'll have to have a *Shabbat* table," he decided. And he made one. The legs were two forked pieces of driftwood stuck in the sand in front of his house. The top was made from a long smooth piece of driftwood. K'tonton also made two driftwood stools, one for himself and an extra one in case a Sabbath guest happened along. He wished he had a white cloth to cover his table, but had to be satisfied with a large, light-colored leaf.

Now for wine and *hallah*.

A wild grapevine climbed over a shrub at the thicket's edge. "If I squeezed juice out of a grape, it would be almost like wine. I could say *Kiddush* over it," K'tonton decided.

But the grapes were tiny green ones, just the beginnings of grapes. The only dark ones he found were hard and wrinkled, like raisins.

Raisins! The word set K'tonton thinking. A raisin is a kind of grape, and there were two raisins in his pocket. They weren't juicy enough to squeeze but they were *pri hagafen*, the fruit of the vine, so it would probably be all right to recite the blessing over them. He didn't think that God would mind if he took a bite instead of a sip.

Encouraged, K'tonton turned his mind to the problem of the *hallah*. An exciting thought came to him. *Matzah* is a kind of bread, unleavened bread, and the children of Israel had baked their *matzah* in the hot sand when they came out of Egypt. There was sand all around him. He would do what the children of Israel had done.

K'tonton had a store of seeds that he had gathered. Now he poured some of them into a tough shell. He had no grinding stones to grind the seeds into flour, the way they did in the days of the Bible, so he pounded them with a tiny pebble from the beach. He pounded until his shoulders ached.

"I guess this will be enough," he decided at last. "The Bible doesn't say that the *matzah* was made out of *fine* flour."

He mixed his flour with rainwater and shaped the dough into two flat cakes. He carried them to the sunniest place he could find and laid them in the sand.

Then he sat down and waited. He waited a very long time, but the cakes didn't bake. All that happened was that sand stuck to them.

"I guess it wasn't such a good idea," K'tonton admitted at last. "Probably the sand in Egypt was hotter than this sand. I'll have to try another way."

Again he pounded grass seeds until they looked a little like flour. This time he poured the flour into two tiny shells, mixed it with water, and shaped it into two loaves. The bread wasn't baked and it wasn't made of wheat or barley. But the grass it had come from had sprung up out of the earth, so K'tonton decided he could recite the blessing over it.

K'tonton set the two loaves on the table in front of the raisins, picked a clover blossom and a daisy for a centerpiece, and tried to think of some way to get Sabbath lights. This time he had to give up. There wasn't anything that he could do.

Would the Sabbath Queen find her way to his house if he didn't have lights?

K'tonton put the worrisome thought out of his mind. He put on his clean shirt, which was now dry, trying not to remem-

ber that this was the hour he would usually be leaving for the synagogue with his father.

It was time to welcome Queen Sabbath. K'tonton arose and turned toward the darkening dunes. He sang:

L'kha dodi.
Come, my beloved, to greet the bride,
Welcome the Sabbath, Queen of the days.

The air had grown still, the sea quiet. Someone was moving through the shadows. Trailing veils of lavender and rose wrapped her round and covered her face.

"The Sabbath Queen!" K'tonton cried, and ran forward to meet her.

"*Bo-i kalah!* Welcome, O bride!" he sang joyfully, bowing low. Twice he bowed. When he looked up the second time, the Queen was gone. Had she left because she found no Sabbath lights on his table? Sadly K'tonton turned toward his house. Then he saw it.

Lights were burning above his table, tiny dancing lights.

When K'tonton had seen those same lights during the week, he had recognized them as fireflies. But now, as they danced over his table, he knew they must be his Sabbath lights.

"The Sabbath Queen left them for me," K'tonton thought in wonder. "She knows that I tried, so she brought me her lights."

He lifted the shell with the two raisins and recited the *Kiddush*, taking a bite of the "fruit of the vine." Then he washed his hands and said *Hamotzi*, the blessing over bread.

His eyes grew wide in astonishment as he took his first bite. The bread didn't taste like grass seeds—it tasted like his mother's *hallah*. He took a second bite. This time it tasted like the tiny fish ball his mother used to make him. Other bites had the taste of noodle soup, of chicken, of pudding. His bread was like the manna that the children of Israel ate in the wilderness:

it had the taste of everything a person wanted. The Sabbath Queen had turned his bread into manna.

The dancing lights were gone, but now the moon shone down. K'tonton sat on at the table, singing all the Sabbath songs his father had taught him. Then he recited his bedtime prayers and crawled into his sleeping bag with a contented smile.

The Sabbath Queen had found him in this strange, far-off place. Maybe his father and mother would find him, too.

K'tonton has a problem

'TONTON was alone on the island in the sea, and he had a problem. The problem was the seat of his pants. The Bible said that the children of Israel wandered in the wilderness for forty years, yet their clothes did not wear out. But K'tonton's pants were wearing out after only a short while on the island. Of course, sliding down sand hills is hard on pants, and K'tonton was always sliding down to the beach, especially when the tide went out. He wanted to see what the waves had left behind. Mostly it was shells or straw or seaweed. But once K'tonton found a piece of white paper he could write on. Another time an old shoe turned up. K'tonton took a sharp piece of broken shell and tried to cut out a piece of leather to make sandals, but the shell didn't work, so he saved the shoelace. "A shoelace can come in handy," he said to himself. He used the shoe to keep things in.

What K'tonton most wanted to find was a bottle. If he could

find a bottle with a cork, he would write a note on the paper, put it inside the bottle, cork the bottle up tight, and push it out into the sea. The note would ask the finder please to let his parents know that he was safe. He would be careful to write down their address and to tell just where he was so that they could come get him. But no bottle turned up. All that happened was that the seat of K'tonton's pants got thinner and thinner.

K'tonton rested on a shell in the wet sand. He thought of other people who had had the same problem. There was a man named Robinson Crusoe who was shipwrecked and had to live alone on an island for years and years. K'tonton's friend David had a book about him. Robinson Crusoe made clothes out of skins, but he had a gun and gunpowder and tools that he had saved from the wreck. K'tonton had nothing.

And there was Simeon bar Yochai, whom his father always told him about on Lag b'Omer. Rabbi Simeon lived a long time ago in the Land of Israel. Wicked Roman soldiers tried to put him in prison because he taught the Torah, but he escaped and hid in a cave for thirteen years. When his clothes wore out, he covered himself with sand.

"Being buried in sand would be fun for a little while," K'tonton thought, "but thirteen years!"

Besides, Simeon bar Yochai didn't have to run around searching for food and water the way K'tonton did. God made a carob tree and a fountain of water spring up at the mouth of the cave. All Rabbi Simeon had to do was to sit on the floor and write his important book, the *Zohar*.

K'tonton cupped his chin in his hands and tried to think of another way out.

"Maybe I can make a pair of pants out of my suit jacket," K'tonton thought, though not very happily. He liked his new suit. "But pants are more important than a jacket."

How could he make a pair of pants without scissors or a needle and thread?

K'tonton was still puzzling over his problem, a worry line in his forehead, when a scraping sound made him look down.

A funny naked crab was backing into an empty snail shell. It looked so comical that K'tonton laughed out loud.

"So that's how *you* get new pants," he said to the crab, still laughing.

The laughing made K'tonton feel better.

"A person can't solve every problem," he told himself. "I'll just stop worrying about my pants. Maybe by the time a hole wears through, Mother and Father will find me."

A Shavuot party
on the island

T was Shavuot, the holiday celebrating God's gift of the Torah to Israel. K'tonton had prepared a Shavuot party, but not for people. There were no other people on the island. The party was to be for his neighbors, Mouse, Rabbit, Turtle, Toad, and the birds. After all, didn't he learn that all God's creatures were present at the giving of the Torah?

K'tonton didn't know the proper form of invitation for a Shavuot party, so he borrowed words from the Passover holiday:

> Let all who are hungry come and eat.
> Let all who are lonely celebrate the festival with me.

Then he sat down quietly and waited.

His house was beautiful with Shavuot greens. Freshly cut grasses covered the floor. Clover and daisies hung from the ceiling. Outside, a rope of honeysuckle vine with sweet-smelling blossoms twined around the tail of his house. Refreshments were set out in front in shells and in heaps: seeds of many kinds, the soft and juicy shoots of young plants, clover blossoms for the bees, gray waxy berries, a few dried-up grapes left over from the year before, a shell filled with tiny rounds of cheese. The rounds weren't real cheese—they were only the flat fruits from a wild plant that children *call* "cheese." K'tonton had often picked them in vacant lots near his home.

"You're supposed to eat cheese on Shavuot," he reminded himself when he found the plants at the edge of the woods. "Cheese blintzes, cheesecake, plain cheese. I'll serve these instead."

K'tonton had also found a bed of wild strawberries, tiny ones, very red and sweet. But these were still inside his house. He couldn't get himself to share them. Strawberries were his favorite dessert. For guests who might want a drink, he had filled up two big shells from his precious store of water.

The first guest to arrive was Mouse. She poked her head out of the tunnel, ran forward a few steps, then back again. Once more she stuck out her head. This time she ran straight to the refreshments and began nibbling at a stalk. Suddenly K'tonton heard a tiny, thin squeak. The squeak wasn't coming from Mouse. It came from underneath Mouse. The mother had brought three babies with her, very tiny and pink, clinging to her body. K'tonton was too excited to keep quiet.

"So *that's* why I haven't seen you around recently!" he exclaimed. "You were having your babies."

Mouse only turned and scurried away.

Next Rabbit hopped up. K'tonton watched as she examined one dish, then another, her nose wiggling. She chose a juicy green stalk and ran off, her powder-puff tail bobbing.

The sun had risen. K'tonton picked up the fringes of his *arba kanfot* and began chanting his prayers. From the grass, the thicket, the beach, voices joined in, chirping, twittering, trilling.

Now the birds began coming. First the little ones he called "neighbors" that lived in the tall grass near his house. (They were little compared to the gulls that flew over the island, but they were not little compared to K'tonton.) The father, handsome in a black collar, black whiskers, and two tiny black horns, led the way. His wife and young ones followed. They didn't fly to the table. They walked quickly on short legs.

Tsweet, tsweet! they lisped as they helped themselves to the grass seeds.

Meow!

K'tonton looked up, startled. Was there a cat in the thicket? He turned protectingly toward the birds. But it wasn't a cat that mewed. It was a slender, gray bird *imitating* a cat. The bird burst into a mocking, rollicking tune as if laughing at K'tonton

for being fooled. The bird flew down, took a sip of water, picked up a berry, and took off again.

Birds were now coming from all directions, hopping, flying, flirting their tails, dipping their wings in the water and shaking drops on one another. Some ate the berries, some the seeds, some only tasted the water.

All morning they came in twos and threes and flocks. K'tonton had to refill the shells over and over again. There were tiny birds with crowns of gold on their heads, gray little birds with topknots, a yellow bird with a black mask over his eyes. "He's masquerading," K'tonton decided. "He's made a mistake

and thinks this is Purim." There were sober brown little birds with tipped-up tails. Others were gay with color: blue, red, yellow, orange, purple. It looked to K'tonton as if a rainbow had broken into bits and the bits were flying.

It was past noon before K'tonton remembered that he had not yet eaten. He went into his house for dinner. He ate a bit of seed bread, two cheeses—and a strawberry. The strawberry was delicious, but eating it made K'tonton feel uncomfortable.

"Greedy! That's what you are!" he scolded himself. "Inviting guests to a party and keeping the best food for yourself."

Ashamed, he filled one of the shells outside with the rest of the strawberries. At that moment Turtle plodded up.

Turtle made straight for the strawberries. When K'tonton offered him some, he ate until not one berry was left. Crunch, crunch, crunch! His mouth was red with crushed berries. After he finished he looked up at K'tonton as if apologizing for the empty dish.

"I understand," K'tonton reassured him. "I almost ate them all myself."

Dusk was falling when the last visitor arrived. K'tonton, standing near the water shell, felt something brush his hand. A toad had hopped up. K'tonton jumped back. His friend Sammy had told him that toads give you warts. Then he remembered that David, who was a cub scout, said this wasn't true. Toads, David said, are people's friends.

The toad was sipping water from the shell. K'tonton bent over and made himself pat him right on his warty bumps. Toad didn't hop away. He looked up at K'tonton out of his orange eyes as if he was pleased to be patted.

The party was over at last. K'tonton's store of food was all gone. Most of the water was gone too. But K'tonton was too happy to worry. He felt that he belonged. Mouse, Rabbit, birds, Turtle, Toad, and K'tonton were all one family.

K'tonton leaves the island

TWO days after Tisha b'Av, K'tonton stood on a clump of seaweed at the water's edge, thinking. What he was thinking about was Adam in the Bible. Before he had come to the island, K'tonton had wondered why God said about Adam, "It is not good for man to be alone." Adam wasn't alone—didn't he have all the animals to keep him company? Now K'tonton understood. Toad and Turtle were his good friends. He had grown fond of Mouse and the rabbits, even of Bat and her baby. And there were the birds. But K'tonton wanted his own kind. He wanted his friends, David and Sammy. He wanted his father and mother.

K'tonton looked across the water to the far shore where he had left them almost three months before. Twice—on the Sabbaths before the two new moons—he had prayed: "May the wishes of my heart be fulfilled for good." But the biggest wish of his heart had not been fulfilled. Would he ever see his father and mother again? K'tonton began to recite one verse, then another, to comfort himself:

> The Lord is with me, I shall not fear.
> Is anything too hard for the Lord?

If God wanted to, He could return him to his father's house in a minute.

He was repeating the verses for the seventh time when he noticed that the clump of seaweed on which he was standing had broken loose. It was the kind of seaweed that had air pockets to make it float. He was moving across the water on a seaweed raft! This time there were no waves or wind, only tiny sparkles and a gentle swell.

Sea birds were following him, the slender black-capped kind with forked tails. They hovered above the sea, their orange feet dangling, then dove down, rose again, fluttering their wings, never resting. K'tonton felt his own heart flutter. Was God answering his prayers? He was moving toward the very shore from which the gull had carried him. Once he reached it, he would surely find someone who would take him home. But suppose a sudden wind arose, the way it had the other time? K'tonton shut his eyes and began to say the verse again:

> The Lord is with me, I shall not fear.
> The Lord is with me, I shall not fear.

Seven times he repeated it. Then he felt the raft dip. The swell curved over into a wave and deposited him on the beach.

K'tonton opened his eyes. He was lying on the sand. Voices came to him from above.

K'tonton knew the people speaking. The man was his own doctor from home. The woman was Mrs. W., who put his adventures in a book.

"Dr. Schwartz! Dr. Schwartz!" K'tonton called. "It's me, K'tonton."

"K'tonton!" Dr. Schwartz stooped down and stared. "It's a good thing you called," he said. "I'd have mistaken you for a bundle of straw."

"It's my poncho," K'tonton explained. "I left my jacket in the house with the tail."

"A house with a tail!" Mrs. W. reached for her notebook. "What—"

Dr. Schwartz interrupted her. "The story can wait. Now I've got to get this young one home to his parents. They've worried about him long enough."

He glanced at his watch. "If we hurry we can make the one

o'clock train. Don't look so sober," he said to K'tonton. "I'm here for a convention, but I'll skip the last meeting. You'll be home in time for *Shabbat.*"

"Do you know which *Shabbat* it is?" he asked, as he picked K'tonton up.

"*Shabbat Nachamu*, the Sabbath of Comfort," K'tonton answered.

"Right! And having you home will make it a real Sabbath of Comfort for your folks."

He stuck K'tonton into his vest pocket. "You won't travel in a hatband this time," he said. "If the wind wants to carry you away, it will have to take me too."

K'tonton couldn't help laughing at the thought of the wind carrying off stout Dr. Schwartz.

"You didn't call me, but I thought I'd stop by," Dr. Schwartz said when K'tonton's father opened the door. His mother was close behind. "I found something at the convention that's sure to cure what's wrong with you."

Dr. Schwartz drew something out of his pocket. There, standing on his hand, safe and well and smiling joyfully, was their loving, long-lost K'tonton.

K'tonton goes to Israel

HOW did K'tonton happen to come to the Land of Israel? It had all begun the day before in his friend David's house. At the time he was sitting behind a candlestick high up on the mantelpiece. K'tonton had chosen the place so that he might see what was going on. David's house was full of visitors, friends, and relatives who had come to say goodbye to David's Aunt Minnie. Mrs. Levy—Aunt Minnie—was going to Israel for Passover. She wanted to celebrate the festival in Jerusalem as people did in the time of the Bible.

"I wish *I* were going, Minnie," one of the cousins said. "Can't you take me along in your suitcase?" He pointed through the bedroom door to the suitcases piled on the floor.

"Crawl in," said Aunt Minnie, laughing.

Everybody laughed with her—*except K'tonton*. An exciting thought popped into K'tonton's head. He could get into the suitcase, even into the smallest one. That was the lucky part of being thumb-sized. He could slip into the suitcase and go up to the Land of Israel. On Passover he wouldn't say, "Next year in Jerusalem!" as he always had. He would *be* in Jerusalem!

K'tonton hurried across the mantel to the window and slid down the window drape to the floor. It took no more than a minute to reach the pile of luggage in the bedroom. The smallest bag, a cloth one with a zipper, was still open. Now to climb inside! K'tonton hurried to the far end of the room—to get a start—and made a running jump, right into the crease in the bag where the zipper began. He was taking hold of the leather tab, when he remembered something. *He hadn't asked his father and mother for permission.*

"But if I wait to ask permission, David's aunt will be gone," K'tonton thought.

He considered the matter. "Father says, 'If the chance to do a good deed, a *mitzvah*, comes to you, do it at once. Don't delay.' Going up to Jerusalem is a very big *mitzvah*. It says so in the Bible. Father wouldn't want me to put it off. I'll leave a letter for him and explain."

He slid to the floor again. A piece of white wrapping paper was lying nearby. K'tonton took a tiny pencil out of his pocket. It was really a bit of lead broken off from a pencil. In thin spidery letters he wrote:

Dear Father and Mother,

   I have found a way to go up to the Land of Israel so I am going. Please excuse me for not saying goodbye. There is no time, because the way I am going is in David's aunt's bag. It is a *mitzvah* to go up to Jerusalem for Passover, so I knew you would not mind. As soon as I arrive, I will send you a letter.

From me, your loving son,
K'tonton

P.S. Do not worry that I will be hungry, Mother. My pockets are full of David's mother's honey cake.

K'tonton folded the paper, wrote on the outside in the big-gest letters he could:

DEAR DAVID, PLEASE GIVE THIS NOTE TO MY FATHER

and pinned it to a footstool.

Then he leaped back into the fold of the bag and slipped inside. Just in time!

"The taxi is here," someone called.

The zipper was pulled shut, the bag lifted.

K'tonton was on his way.

K'tonton goes up to Jerusalem

K'TONTON was in Israel. He had just arrived and was standing outside the airport. "Abraham may have once stood on this very spot," K'tonton thought. "Or King David, or Rabbi Akiba."

K'tonton wanted to see the whole country. He looked for a car to take him around. Then he saw the perfect one. It was a very old car. The fender, bent and battered, almost reached the ground, so that K'tonton could reach it and hoist himself up. The dents in the metal gave him a foothold. The upholstery inside had torn places for his fingers to dig into. Up the back of the rear seat, K'tonton climbed. At the top, quite close to the window, was a perfect hole.

"I can hide in here and get a good view at the same time," K'tonton thought, as he fitted himself inside.

Mind you, K'tonton didn't need to hide. Every Jew is welcome in the State of Israel. But it seemed easier to K'tonton to hide than to explain how he had come to Israel.

The driver came up, threw a number of packages into the trunk of the car, then got in. The engine coughed and chugged. The car was on its way. Only K'tonton and the driver were inside. The rest of the tourists had chosen the shiny cars ahead.

Zoom, rattle, bang! The car sped down the road, then lurched around a corner. They were climbing into the hills, in and out along a corkscrew road. A signpost caught K'tonton's eye.

K'tonton's heart leaped.

"We're going up to Jerusalem," it sang, "to Jerusalem, where the Holy Temple stood. It's like it says in the Psalms:

I rejoiced when they said to me,
'Let us go up to the House of the Lord.'

Only I'm not *saying* it . . . I'm *doing* it!"

The song in K'tonton's heart rose up and up. He couldn't hold it back. It burst from his lips, thin, and sweet, and clear.

The driver heard it and turned. There on top of the rear seat, his feet fitted snugly in a hole in the upholstery, stood a tiny, thumb-sized boy.

"Shalom!" said the driver, looking interested but not surprised. He was used to seeing all kinds of Jews in Israel—blond Jews, black Jews, giant Jews from the Caucasus, brown lean Yemenite Jews with side curls, cave-dwelling Jews. This was a thumb-sized Jew.

"Shalom!" he said again. "Why do you sit there by yourself?" He grinned down at K'tonton. "The front seat upholstery also has good holes."

Without slowing down, he stretched out an arm to make a bridge for K'tonton to cross over.

From the top of the front seat, K'tonton looked up into the man's face. It was a pleasant face, browned by the sun and weather, with a nice big nose and blue eyes with wrinkles under them. "For the smiles to run down," K'tonton thought. The man's shirt was open at the neck. A beret was tipped back from his forehead.

"And where do you come from?" he asked, one eye on K'tonton, the other on the road, which at that moment was making a hairpin turn.

"I'm going up to Jerusalem," K'tonton said. He knew that this wasn't an answer to the question, but at the moment where he was going seemed more important than where he had come from.

The hills grew steeper and more barren. Stones and boulders covered them. Suddenly K'tonton pointed excitedly. Men with pickaxes were splitting huge rocks.

"The stones! Are they iron?" K'tonton asked.

"Iron?"

K'tonton answered with a Bible verse:

A land whose stones are iron and out of whose hills you may dig brass.

"I see you know your Bible," said the driver. "That makes you half an Israeli already. The stones you are talking about are down in the Negev near King Solomon's mines."

"Do you mean King Solomon who built the Holy Temple?" K'tonton's voice was filled with awe.

"The very one! They're digging copper out of those old mines right now."

He was going to tell about the discovery of the ancient mines, but K'tonton's eyes were again on the hills. The dead, gray stones were gone. Grapevines rose in terraces. Pine trees covered the hill tops. Barns and neat red-roofed houses hid among green orchards.

"Trees!" K'tonton said in wonder. "Hills covered with trees! Maybe those are the ones the coins from my blue-and-white box paid for. Maybe my tree that was planted when I was born is up there?"

He climbed out of the hole and leaned out of the window to get a better view.

A pull at his shirt brought him back.

"Easy there!" said the driver. "You're not trying to leave me, are you? I thought you wanted to go up to Jerusalem."

His blue eyes looked into K'tonton's dark eyes that were shining like stars.

"What did you say your name was?" he asked.

"I didn't say," K'tonton answered. "It's Isaac Samuel ben Baruch Reuben, for short K'tonton." Then in the same breath, "Are those Jewish National Fund trees? Are there any almond trees up there? Do you think there might be one my age, because . . ."

The man's eyes were laughing. "So your name is K'tonton. You ask so many questions. I thought your name was Question Mark."

He pointed to a grove of olive trees ahead. Through the silvery tops rose the towers of Jerusalem. The car turned a corner.

"We're here, K'tonton," the driver said. "Where do you want to get off?"

They were on a noisy crowded street. People hurried in and out of stores, stood in long lines on the corners. Buses and taxis honked.

Suddenly Jerusalem seemed to K'tonton very big and strange, very far from home.

"I'll get off at . . . at . . ." he hesitated.

"Because," the driver went on, "if you haven't any special place to go to, you could come home with me." He brought the car to a stop. "My wife would enjoy a guest for Passover. You are so good at asking questions, you could ask the *Mah nishtanah*." He meant the Four Questions the youngest child of the family asks on Passover Eve.

"Don't you have a son to ask?" K'tonton's eyes were filled with sympathy.

"Oh, I have a son all right, a fine, smart child," the driver assured him. "But he can't manage the *Mah nishtanah* by himself. He's only a year and a half old."

"My father has one son, too." K'tonton said gravely. "Me. I don't know who will ask *him* the *Mah nishtanah* this year."

Suddenly a tear slid down K'tonton's cheek and caught in a corner of his mouth. He sucked it in quickly.

That night K'tonton wrote to his parents. He wrote about his flight and everything that had happened to him since he arrived in the Holy Land. Their answer came before Passover. "We are glad you have found friends in Israel," the letter said. "You may stay until we save enough money for tickets. Then we will come and join you."

A Passover mix-up

K'TONTON was in Jerusalem. He was spending Passover with the driver Shimshon, his wife Hannah, and their son Raphael.

"I don't know how I'd get my Passover cleaning done without K'tonton," Hannah said to Shimshon. "He's a bigger help to me than *you* are."

"Name one thing K'tonton can do that I can't."

"Can *you* crawl into the coat pockets to look for crumbs?" Hannah asked. "And he's so good with Raphael."

"Say *Mah nishtanah halailah hazeh,* Raphael," K'tonton urged.

"*Abba mah,*" Raphael began. Then he stopped and grinned up at his father.

"That's as far as he'll go," K'tonton explained, apologetically. "I guess I'm not a very good teacher. He'll never be ready in time for the *seder.*" The *seder,* the home celebration on the first night of Passover, was only two days off.

"Raphael won't have to ask the *Mah nishtanah* this year," said Hannah. "We're going to the family *seder*. There'll be plenty of cousins to do the asking."

A look of dismay came into K'tonton's face.

"You'll come with us, of course, K'tonton," Hannah hurried to explain. "Did you think we'd leave you behind?"

But it wasn't the fear of being left behind that troubled K'tonton. It was the thought of all the new people he would have to meet.

"Could I go in Raphael's pocket?" he asked. Hannah had made Raphael a new suit for Passover, a real boy's suit with two pockets. "Raphael likes me to be near him. And . . . and . . ." K'tonton blurted it out. "If I went in his pocket, I'd be at the *seder* but nobody would know I was there."

"You can go any way you like," Hannah assured him. And that was how the mix-up came about.

The *seder* was at Shimshon's father's house. It was a low stone house with a garden in front and a tiled floor inside. When they came in, Shimson's mother was standing near the long table, arranging the pillows for his father to lean on. She dropped everything and gave Raphael a warm hug, K'tonton, hidden in Raphael's pocket, could feel the hug. It was just like his mother's. He almost climbed out to wish Raphael's grandmother a happy Passover. Then he looked around at all the aunts and uncles and cousins, taking their places at the table, and he was glad he hadn't climbed out. There was a stern-looking uncle in a fur hat and a silk coat. There was an uncle in a frock coat and skull cap, and another like Shimshon in a white shirt and no tie. There were girl cousins and boy cousins. The youngest one was practicing the *Mah nishtanah* under his breath. The grandfather called him Meirke.

Then the service began and K'tonton forgot all about the company. It was exactly like his father's *seder*. K'tonton knew the words so well, he had to be careful not to say them out loud.

First the *Kiddush*, the blessing over the wine; then "Let all who are hungry come and eat"; then greens dipped in salt water. K'tonton managed to nibble a tiny bit of Raphael's.

Then the grandfather turned toward Raphael. There was a twinkle like Shimshon's in his eyes.

"Well, Raphael," he said, "are you ready to ask the *Mah nishtanah?* You're the youngest, you know."

Everybody smiled. The next minute the smiles turned to amazement. From Raphael's place a voice was rising, thin but sweet and clear: "*Mah nishtanah halailah hazeh mikol halaylot?*"

(Why is this night different from all other nights?) Raphael the *baby* was asking the *Mah nishtanah*. Who had ever heard of such a wonder?

Only Hannah and Shimshon knew that the voice was K'tonton's, not Raphael's. Mind you, K'tonton had not meant to speak. It was just that he was so used to asking the Four Questions. When the proper moment came, he had spoken up without thinking. Now he crouched down in Raphael's pocket, dismayed at the thing that he had done. He wished that he could hide forever.

The family was waiting breathlessly for Raphael to go on. K'tonton could see them through one eye. Clearest of all, he could see Meirke. A tear was running down Meirke's cheek. *He* had expected to ask the *Mah nishtanah*. He had practiced it.

"Now he can't ask on account of me," K'tonton thought in distress. "And it's his right to ask. Except for Raphael, he's the youngest at the table."

K'tonton's head was whirling. He looked pleadingly toward Shimshon. Shimshon's lips formed the words, "Shall I tell?"

K'tonton nodded yes.

Shimshon threw him a quick smile, then turned toward his father.

"Father, family," he said, "I am flattered that you think our Raphael is already a *chacham*, but the truth is that he is still a *she'ayno yodaya lishol*.

In the Passover Haggadah the *chacham* is the wise child. The *she'ayno yodaya lishol* is the child who isn't able to ask.

Shimshon continued. "We have a guest at our *seder*. It was he who began to ask the questions—by mistake." He lifted K'tonton out of Raphael's pocket and set him on the table. "It gives me great pleasure to present K'tonton ben Baruch Reuben, a recent arrival in Israel."

A gasp ran around the table. A thumb-sized guest! This was

even more amazing than having a baby ask the Four Questions. Every eye in the room was on K'tonton.

But K'tonton was too relieved to mind. Meirke had arisen and was asking the *Mah nishtanah.* Straight through the Four Questions he went, his voice filled with happiness. But not even Meirke was as happy as K'tonton. The wrong he hadn't meant to do had been righted.

Wisdom from a donkey

**K**'TONTON walked along a lane between high stone walls. The smile, which had been growing wider and wider since the day he arrived in Israel, had suddenly disappeared. A frown puckered his forehead. At whom was he frowning? At *himself*.

"Here I am," he thought, "come at last to the Land of Israel. All around me is work waiting to be done, stones to gather, rocks to crush, swamps to drain, deserts to water, forests to plant, houses to build. I should have been a giant. And what am I? A K'tonton!"

He squinted his eyes upward, then glanced down.

"Four inches from his head to toe," he said in disgust. "What can I do with four inches?"

At that moment K'tonton noticed a donkey. It was hitched to an oil cart near a gate in the stone wall. While its master was in the houses delivering the oil, the donkey cropped the weeds that grew beside the road.

It was the weeds that caught K'tonton's eye. They were thistles, tall prickly thistles. How could the donkey eat thistles without getting the prickles in its tongue? Curiosity made K'tonton forget his worries. If there was one thing in K'tonton that wasn't tiny, it was his curiosity. He went closer to the donkey to get a better look. Then he remembered that the donkey might gobble him up along with the thistles. Not deliberately! Donkeys are vegetarians. But because he was so small the donkey might gobble him up by accident.

A bougainvillea vine, bright with blossoms, covered the wall. K'tonton took hold of a branch. Up and up he climbed, then sprang lightly to the donkey's back. Running the length of its back was easy. Climbing downhill along its bent neck was harder, but K'tonton made it. By kneeling between its long ears and leaning forward, he could look straight down the donkey's nose to its mouth. K'tonton watched intently as the tongue came out. It was hard and leathery.

"So that's why you can eat thistles! You have a leather tongue." K'tonton laughed aloud, pleased with himself for having solved the puzzle.

Maybe it was the laughter that startled the donkey. Maybe K'tonton had stepped on a ticklish place between its ears. Suddenly it lifted its head and opened its jaws wide. Out came a squeaking hee, followed by a tremendous HAW—a giant haw, an earth-shaking—at least a K'tonton-shaking—HAW. K'tonton tumbled down among the thistles.

"And *my* skin isn't leathery," he thought, as the thistles pricked and scratched his cheeks.

A second hee-HAW followed. This one had a reproachful sound. The donkey was looking directly at K'tonton. It seemed to be talking to him.

"Maybe the donkey *is* talking to me," K'tonton thought, "the way the donkey talked to Balaam in the Bible. The Bible says it spoke, but it doesn't say what language it spoke. Maybe it was donkey language. Maybe this donkey has a message for *me*."

A third time the donkey opened its mouth wide and brayed. Its tongue showed clearly, dark and hard and leathery.

This time K'tonton understood. The donkey was saying, "You ought to be ashamed of yourself, K'tonton, complaining about your size. God gave *me* a leathery tongue. Do I complain? No! I use it to clear the land of thistles. *If you have no bigness to help with, help with your littleness!*"

"Thank you, donkey. That's just what I'll do," K'tonton said humbly.

He crawled out of the clump of thistles, too excited to feel the scratches. "I'll search," he said, "until I find a way."

The very next day K'tonton discovered the clinic. He hid inside the half-opened cover of a tourist's camera bag. When the tourist visited the clinic, so did K'tonton.

The grownups in the clinic waited patiently, thinking anxious thoughts. The children wiggled and pulled at their mothers' skirts. They didn't like waiting. A tousle-headed boy climbed over a bench and got a spanking from his father. He opened his mouth and bawled. "Ow—w—w—ow—!" Two little sisters in pink starched dresses bawled in sympathy. A baby, frightened by the noise, began crying. A little Arab girl, bangles on her forehead, looked as if she were going to cry too. So did a sad-eyed boy with side curls peeking out beneath a bandage on his head. *All* the children began crying.

A pretty nurse in a ponytail hurried in, but she couldn't stop them. The fathers and mothers couldn't stop them.

Suddenly, the children stopped by themselves. The tousle-headed boy, who had started the trouble, began laughing instead of crying. The sad-eyed boy with the bandaged head smiled. The Arab girl put her hand to her mouth—the good hand that wasn't in a sling—and stared, her eyes under the

bangles full of wonder. The sisters in the pink starched dresses laughed out loud. *All* the children were laughing.

The parents sighed with relief. The nurse with the ponytail laughed. "It's as catching as the measles," she said to a doctor who had opened his door to see what the commotion was about. "One child bawls, they all begin bawling. A child laughs . . . and look at them! You'd think they were watching a circus."

The grownups didn't know it, but the children *were* watching a circus, or rather a circus clown. He was a tiny clown, no more than four inches tall, and he didn't wear a clown's suit. But he did handsprings and somersaults and flip-flops like a clown. He was so funny, the children couldn't help laughing. They didn't mind waiting their turn any more. They didn't even want their turn to come.

The clown, of course, was K'tonton. He had arrived at the clinic and managed to get out of the camera case just as the crying began. He almost joined in the crying. Then he remembered how long ago, on a Purim day, he had made a sad, sick-in-bed little boy laugh. The first thing he knew, he was turning cartwheels and somersaults to make the children laugh.

All the rest of the day K'tonton kept watch on the children from a hiding-place under a bench. At the first sight of a frown, he ran out and performed.

K'tonton had learned a lesson from the donkey. The donkey used his leathery tongue to clear the land of thistles, and K'tonton used his littleness to cheer sick children. From then on, K'tonton kept finding new ways to serve with his littleness.

Size isn't everything

K'TONTON was in Haifa. Below him were the blue waters of the harbor. Big ships lay at anchor. He looked up. The city had climbed a mountain. White houses, sparkling in the sun, peeked from between cool pine trees and bright gardens.

K'tonton's heart beat fast. This was Mount Carmel. At the top of the mountain was the Technion, the school with the wonderful machine K'tonton had heard about. One of the many people K'tonton had met in Israel told him that the Technion had a microscope that made small things big.

A student was standing at the curbstone, trying to hitch a ride up the Carmel. He had set down a package he was carrying. K'tonton slipped into the wrappings—where the paper folded over—just as a small compact car came to a stop. The student picked up the package and hopped in, not knowing that he was taking with him another hitchhiker, a thumb-sized one.

So it was that K'tonton arrived at the Technion, and was left in a package on a desk in a sunny office.

A sign on the desk read:

A. CARL

K'tonton heard a door shut with a bang, then open again. He looked for a moment. Then he slipped out of the wrappings of the package and looked up—into a man's startled eyes. The startled look quickly changed to a smile of welcome.

"Is there anything I can do for you?" Mr. Carl asked.

"My name is K'tonton. I'm from America. If you please, could you take me to the machine that makes little things big?" K'tonton glanced at the slip of paper in his jacket. "You call it . . . mic . . . microscope. It *is* here, isn't it?"

"We have many microscopes here," said Mr. Carl. "What do you want a microscope for?"

"So I can get big," K'tonton answered, surprised that Mr. Carl should ask. "I've heard that if you put something very small on the big glass shelf and look through a kind of tube, the small thing gets big. Please, sir," K'tonton said eagerly, "will you put *me* on the glass so I can grow big?"

Mr. Carl picked up K'tonton in his hand. "K'tonton," he said gently, "I'm afraid you don't quite understand what a microscope does. The little thing on the slide—slide is what we call the glass shelf—the little thing doesn't really get big. It just *looks* big. When you take it off the glass, it's as small as before. Besides, you're too big to fit on the glass. The things we look at through a microscope are so tiny we couldn't even *see* them without the microscope."

Disappointment choked K'tonton's throat, looked out of his eyes.

"Why do you want to be big?" Mr. Carl asked. "I like you as you are."

K'tonton blinked back a tear. "Because if I were big I would be able to do big things."

"I know some *little* things that can do big things," said Mr. Carl. "Come! Let me introduce you to them."

So K'tonton began what Mr. Carl called his "special course at the Technion."

"Lesson One," said Mr. Carl, as he carried K'tonton into a big room he called a biology lab. It was after school hours, and the students had all left.

"There's the microscope you're so interested in," Mr. Carl said, and he set K'tonton down on a table near something with a stand, a long tube, and a little glass shelf. K'tonton saw at once that he could not have fitted on the glass. It was comforting to know that he was too *big* for something, but not comforting enough to make up for his dreadful disappointment. He had so wanted to be big.

"Look at this slide, K'tonton." Mr. Carl pointed to the oblong glass.

K'tonton looked. All he saw was a drop of water.

"Now look at it through the microscope."

Mr. Carl held K'tonton up to the lens and K'tonton pressed an eye against it. The drop of water turned into a pond with tiny wriggling creatures swimming around.

"Do you know what these tiny creatures can do?" said Mr. Carl. "They can make a strong man sick. And these"—he pointed to another slide— "can make a sick man well."

K'tonton hardly heard him. He was too busy being sorry for himself because the microscope couldn't help *him*.

"Maybe Lesson Two will go better," said Mr. Carl. "We'll try the Mining Engineering Department."

He carried K'tonton into another building. Specimens of rocks and metals of every kind and color were arranged on shelves.

"Which do you think is the most precious?" Mr. Carl asked.

K'tonton didn't answer.

"That one is." Mr. Carl pointed to the smallest stone of all. "It's a diamond."

"I know," said K'tonton. "You put diamonds in rings."

"And in watches to make them go and in machines to drill and to grind. These tiny stones can cut the hardest rock."

K'tonton was no longer listening.

"Well, there's still Lesson Three," said Mr. Carl hopefully.

This time he carried K'tonton across the campus to a lecture hall in a fine new building.

K'tonton saw rows and rows of seats. Up front was a desk with a blackboard behind it. A chalk diagram with big and little circles and pointing lines was drawn on the blackboard.

"That's a drawing of something we call an atom," Mr. Carl said, "but a million, billion times bigger than it really is. You know the size of a toy balloon?"

K'tonton nodded.

"Well, you could put a hundred million billion atoms in one toy balloon. That's how tiny they are. And do you know what those tiny atoms will do for us when our students learn how to put them to work? They'll make electricity for our homes and our factories. They'll run our ships. They'll help doctors make people well. They'll even move mountains, if we want them to!"

This time K'tonton's eyes were sparkling with excitement.

"That's what atoms can do," Mr. Carl went on. "And they're so tiny you can't see them even with a microscope—not even with an electronic microscope. That's the most powerful kind of all. Do you still think little things can't do big important work?"

It would have been better if Mr. Carl had not mentioned the microscope. The word set K'tonton thinking again about his big mistake. The sparkle left his eyes.

Mr. Carl looked discouraged for a moment. Then a gleam

ALBANIA
YUGOSLAVIA
BULGARIA
U. S. S. R.
GREECE
BLACK SEA
AEGEAN SEA
TURKEY
MEDITERRANEAN SEA
CYPRUS
SYRIA
LEBANON
ISRAEL
JORDAN
IRAQ
IRAN
EGYPT
NILE
SAUDI ARABIA
RED SEA
KUWAIT
PERSIAN GULF
SUDAN

came into his eyes. Back across the campus he went, K'tonton tucked into his pocket. Students nodded to him as he passed. A tall professor stopped to ask if he could spare a few minutes. There was something he wanted to discuss. Mr. Carl asked him if it could wait until the next day. He had an important visitor from America.

Back in his office, Mr. Carl took a map out of a drawer and spread it wide on his desk. It was a map of the world.

"K'tonton," Mr. Carl said, setting him down on the map, "can you find America for me?"

K'tonton found it.

"Europe? Asia? Africa?"

K'tonton found them all.

"Now the Mediterranean Sea," said Mr. Carl.

K'tonton found the Mediterranean Sea, and many countries on the shores of the sea: Italy shaped like a boot, Greece, Turkey, Egypt.

"Where is Israel?" Mr. Carl asked.

Israel was harder to find. It was so tiny. When K'tonton tried to point to it, his finger touched its neighbors Lebanon, Syria, and Jordan.

"Hm," said Mr. Carl. "Israel can't be very important. It's just a speck on the map."

"But, Mr. Carl, Israel is *very* important!" K'tonton sprang to Israel's defense. "It's the land God promised to Abraham. The whole Bible came from Israel. And now . . ."

A twinkle in Mr. Carl's eyes made K'tonton stop in the middle of his sentence. Now he knew what Mr. Carl had been trying to teach him.

"I guess size isn't everything," he admitted. And he grinned up at Mr. Carl.

The disappointment in K'tonton's heart had melted away. He and the State of Israel were both K'tontons.

Glossary

abba   the Hebrew word for "father."

arba kanfot   a small vest-like garment with fringes on each of its four corners, worn by very religious Jews as a reminder to keep God's commandments.

aron kodesh   the Holy Ark, a cabinet in the synagogue in which the Torah scrolls (*Sifrei Torah*) are kept.

dreidel   a four-sided spinning top with a different Hebrew letter—*nun, gimel, heh, shin*—on each of its sides. The letters stand for *Nes gadol haya sham* ("What a miracle was there!"). These remind us of the miracle that took place in the Temple of Jerusalem, when the lamp, which had enough oil for only one day, burned for eight days.

Eretz Yisrael   Hebrew for "the Land of Israel."

etrog   a citron, a citrus fruit, carried with the *lulav* and myrtle and willow twigs in the synagogue during the procession at Sukkot.

grogger   a noisemaker used while the *Megillah* is being read at Purim to drown out the name of the wicked Haman.

Haggadah   the book read during the Passover *seder* service. It tells the story of the Jews' Exodus from Egypt and includes prayers and songs.

hallah   a loaf of white bread used on the Sabbath, usually braided. Two are placed on the Sabbath table, covered with a white cloth.

halutzim   Jewish pioneer settlers who built up the Land of Israel.

hamantashen   small cakes, filled with poppyseeds or fruit and eaten at Purim, shaped like Haman's three-cornered hat.

Hamotzi   the blessing over bread, giving thanks to God, "Who brings forth bread from the earth."

Hanukkah   the eight-day holiday celebrating the victory of the Maccabees over the Syrians. The defiled Temple of Jerusalem was rededicated after the victory. Hanukkah lights are kindled on each night of the festival.

Hoshanot   prayers of salvation recited during the Sukkot procession in synagogue.

Kiddush   a prayer said at the Sabbath meal, recited over a cup of wine. In the prayer the wine is called *pri hagafen*, the fruit of the vine.

lulav   the palm branch carried, along with the *etrog*, the myrtle, and the willow twigs, in the Sukkot procession in the synagogue.

Mah nishtanah   the opening words of the Four Questions that are asked, in Hebrew, at the Passover *seder* by the youngest child.

matzah   unleavened bread eaten at Passover.

Megillah   the Scroll of Esther, which is read on Purim.

menorah   the Hanukkah lamp, which holds eight lights.

mitzvah   Hebrew for "commandment." A law of the Torah, telling what to do and what not to do (according to the Talmud there are 613 of them). A *mitzvah* can also be any good or charitable deed.

Negev   the south of Israel, a land of many deserts.

Passover   a festival in spring celebrating the Jews' Exodus from slavery in ancient Egypt.

Purim   the joyous holiday celebrating the deliverance of the Jews from the wicked Haman, who plotted to destroy them.

Rosh Hashanah   The Jewish New Year, observed in the autumn. It is a solemn holiday, when people reflect on their deeds and are judged by God.

Shabbat   the Jewish Sabbath, a day of rest and joy, beginning at sundown on Friday and ending after sundown on Saturday. On Friday evenings, candles are lit, special prayers are recited, good food is eaten, and songs are sung.

Shabbat Nachamu the Sabbath of Comfort, the Sabbath immediately following Tisha b'Av, when the words of the prophet Isaiah are read in the synagogue: "Comfort, oh comfort My people."

seder the traditional Passover meal commemorating the Jews' Exodus from slavery in Egypt.

shalom the Hebrew word for "hello," "goodbye," and "peace."

Shavuot the holiday celebrating the giving of the Ten Commandments on Mount Sinai.

Shema the prayer beginning "Hear, O Israel! The Lord is our God, the Lord alone" (Deuteronomy 6:4-5).

Sukkot the fall festival of thanksgiving, commemorating the Jews' wandering in the desert for forty years. Meals are eaten in the *sukkah,* a shelter with a roof made of branches and leaves.

tallit the prayer shawl with fringes at each corner worn by Jews in the synagogue.

Tisha b'Av the fast day recalling the destruction of the First and Second Temples by the Babylonians and the Romans.

tzedakah righteousness and charity.

Yom Kippur the Day of Atonement, following ten days after Rosh Hashanah, when God seals the fate of mankind for the coming year. It is a solemn day of fasting, prayer, and reflection.

SADIE ROSE WEILERSTEIN was a leading author of Jewish children's books and short stories for over fifty years. Among her books are *What the Moon Brought, Little New Angel, What Danny Did,* and *Ten and a Kid.* K'tonton, the best known of her characters, made his first appearance in a story published in the September 1930 issue of *Outlook* magazine. He subsequently became the hero of three books—*The Adventures of K'tonton, K'tonton in Israel,* and *K'tonton on an Island in the Sea.* Mrs. Weilerstein received a special Jewish Book Council Award for her "cumulative contribution to Jewish juvenile writing" and the Women's League for Conservative Judaism's Yovel award "in recognition of her outstanding and pioneer contributions to the world of books for Jewish children." Subsequent to the publication of *The Best of K'tonton,* a new book, *K'tonton in the Circus: A Hanukkah Adventure,* was published.

MARILYN HIRSH is the author-illustrator of over twenty books for children. Among her books are four that she illustrated in India while serving with the Peace Corps. Her many books of Jewish interest—including *Ben Goes into Business, The Rabbi and the Twenty-Nine Witches,* and *Potato Pancakes All Around*—earned for her the Association of Jewish Libraries 1979 Sydney Taylor Award for her contribution to Jewish children's literature.

FRANCINE KLAGSBRUN is an author, editor, and lecturer. Among her books are *Free To Be . . . You and Me, Too Young To Die: Youth and Suicide,* and *Voices of Wisdom: Jewish Ideals and Ethics for Everyday Living.*